W9-ACD-485

+
Si3920

On Grandma's Roof

Erica Silverman

Illustrated by

Deborah Kogan Ray

Macmillan Publishing Company   New York
Collier Macmillan Publishers   London

Printed and bound in Japan   First American Edition   10 9 8 7 6 5 4 3 2 1

The text of this book is set in 15 point Bembo. The illustrations are rendered in watercolor and pencil.

Library of Congress Cataloging-in-Publication Data   •   Silverman, Erica.
On grandma's roof / Erica Silverman; illustrated by Deborah Kogan Ray. —1st American ed.   p.   cm.
Summary: A little girl describes the fun she has on laundry day on Grandma's roof.
ISBN 0-02-782681-3
[1. Grandmothers—Fiction.   2. Roofs—Fiction.]   I. Ray, Deborah Kogan, date, ill.   II. Title.
PZ7.S586250n   1990   89-31255 CIP AC

To my Mima, Pearl Sheer Phillips,
who gave me the world from her roof,
and her mother, Etel, for whom I am named
and her daughters, Gloria (my mom)
and Marcia (my aunt) — with much love
— E.S.

Remembering Aunt Anna's Roof
— D.K.R.

The stairway up to Grandma's roof is narrow and dark. Grandma carries the laundry. I carry the picnic basket.

"Out we go, Emily!" Grandma pushes, and the roof door swings open.

On Grandma's roof, the bright sun makes me squint. The wind blows my hair into my mouth.

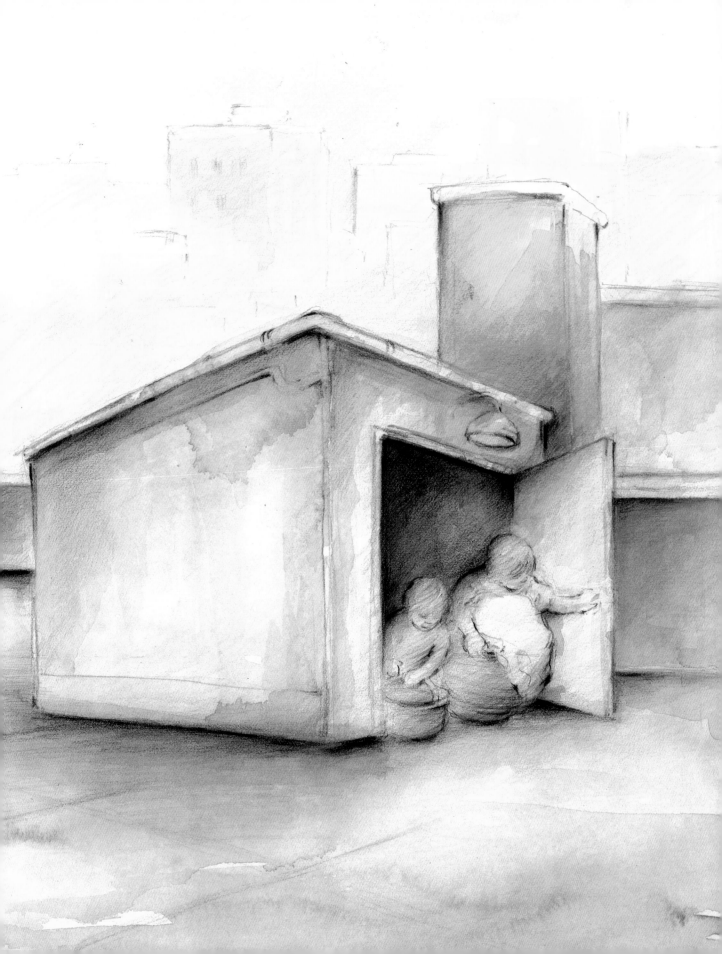

At the clothesline, Grandma puts down the laundry.
I set the picnic basket in the chimney's shade.
Four pigeons waddle over.
"Shoo!" Grandma stomps her foot.
She picks up a shirt. Then she holds out her hand.

I hand her two clothespins. "Here come the wooden
people. This one's Sue and that one's Lou."

"How do you do?" says Grandma. She hangs up
socks and towels, sweaters and pillowcases, dresses
and pants.

I hold a big white sheet while Grandma hangs it up.

"All done," she says.

"Can't find me," I call.
Grandma looks and looks.
I sneak behind the big white sheet. "Boo!"
Grandma jumps.
I chase her in and out of the socks and towels, sweaters and pillowcases, dresses and pants.
"Got you!"
"I've got you, too," says Grandma, and she squeezes me tight.

Then I stretch out my arms and let the wind push me. "I'm dancing with the wind."

"Dance with me," says Grandma.

Around and around we whirl, all over the roof. The wind whooshes. The laundry snaps and flaps. From the street below, horns honk. Someone, somewhere, is playing a piano.

"Enough!" cries Grandma.
"I can't dance anymore!"
   "Now let's be statues," I say.
And we stand very still.
   "Grandma, listen. Do you hear
the clothesline creaking?"
   "It has old bones like me."
   "Grandma, your bones don't creak."
   Grandma laughs. She laughs for a long time.
   I feel grown-up, making Grandma laugh.

Together we spread out a big blanket. I put a heavy brick on one side. Grandma puts an old flowerpot on the other, so it won't blow away.

"Come here, Emily." Grandma gives me soap. She pours water from her washing jar over my hands. Then she washes up, too.

On Grandma's roof, we eat chicken salad sandwiches cut into triangles. We stir lemonade with cinnamon sticks. We munch on sweet juicy cherries. They turn my fingertips red. And I bury the pits in the dirt of the old flowerpot.

"Grandma, I'm planting a cherry tree."

Grandma pours the leftover water from her washing jar into the pot. Then she lies down. I lie beside her. She smells of rose perfume and laundry soap.

After a while, I sit up. "What's burning?" I cover my nose.

"Tar," says Grandma. "They're fixing a hole in the road."

I run to the roof wall. "Where?"

Grandma lifts me up.

I look down at the tops of trees and the tops of cars and the tops of people's heads.

A big green bus screeches to a stop. People carrying briefcases and packages get down. They hurry off in different directions. A man rides his bicycle in and out of a long line of cars. Down the street, the florist takes his flowers inside for the night.

Grandma points. "There's Mr. Inglehopper and his dog, King."

Whenever I see King, I hide. But not now.

"Look, Grandma, I'm taller than King. I'm taller than Mr. Inglehopper."

On Grandma's roof, I'm taller than everyone. I am on top of the world. I can see all the way to the end of the city. The bright orange sun peeks out above a tall building. Clouds, painted pink by the sun's light, drift slowly across the sky.

"It's getting late." Grandma puts me down.

At the clothesline, I touch my nose to a sheet and breathe in the fresh summer air.

Grandma touches a towel. "What do you think?" she asks.

"Dry," I tell her. "Definitely dry."

Grandma takes down the laundry. I put the clothespins back in their bag.

"Grandma, who helped you on laundry day before I was born?"

"Your mom and your uncle Mort."

"Anyone else?"

"Your grandpa did," says Grandma. She stares out across the row of roofs. Then she sighs.

I hug her. "Now you have me."

"You and me," says Grandma. "We are a team."

Grandma carries the laundry. I carry the picnic basket.

Grandma opens the roof door.

"Grandma, wait...." I look back.

The wind is still, and I can't see the sun anymore. The clothesline is empty. Laundry day is over on Grandma's roof.